For Eleanor,
I know you'll love animals and reading about them!
♡ Gramma Ringel

O9-AHV-792

THE ZOO's SECRET

Written & Illustrated
by Lindsey Bell

jam
publishers

THE ZOO'S SECRET
Copyright © 2017 by Lindsey Bell
All rights reserved.

No part of this book may be used or reproduced in any
manner whatsoever without written permission.

Written by Lindsey Bell
Illustrated by Lindsey Bell
Edited by Angie Hodapp and Joshua Viola
Layout by Colton Hoerner

A JAM Publishers Book
Published and distributed by JAM Publishers, LLC
PO Box 298
Erie, CO 80516

ISBN-10: 0-9988265-1-0
ISBN-13: 978-0-9988265-1-6

Joshua Viola, Publisher

10 9 8 7 6 5 4 3 2 1
First Edition: June 2017

Printed in the USA

For Mom

Why are the animals asleep at the
zoo? It's not because they're feeling
blue!

At night, they do things they don't
normally do. Shhh! It's a secret!
Listen close. I'll tell you...

All kinds of critters, from tail to snout, wake up with delight when the moon comes out.

The moon shines down on a curious sight—the animals gazing at its silvery light.

Two giants are dancing! They swing to and fro! Their long necks are tangled in a graceful tango.

One giraffe spins, one twirls on fast feet. They pause for a kiss, and their two noses meet.

Swing-dancing monkeys
zing through the air.
They're vine-swinging
acrobats who fast-step
with flair.

They hoot and they
holler, they monkey
around, they swing
through the night to that
old big-band sound.

The foxes, they trot with charm and pizzazz, joyously dancing to Dixieland jazz.

Their tails entwine as they dip and they bend, they spin 'til their favorite song rolls to an end.

High-flying bats emerge
from the trees, they boogie
and woogie and ride the night
breeze.

They jitter and chatter and
chortle and giggle, their little
wings flap, and their little
ears wiggle.

Owls in masquerade costumes embrace, their dance is a whirlwind of feathers and lace.

They sparkle and glitter, and as they take flight, their colorful masks cast a spell on the night.

The porcupines hokey and pokey
and clap, stepping in, stepping out, as
their little toes tap.

They bob and they turn, their tails
a'swingin', to the left, to the right, and
everyone's singin'.

Synchronized seals swim and spiral and splash, they slip through the water, they flip in a flash!

They leap and they soar, they perform their routine, but their goggles are silly and make quite a scene!

The walruses waltz—it's their turn to dance, so they set their own groove and embrace the romance.

Flippers a'flippin', they twirl and they spin, their waltz is exquisite from tail to fin.

Flamingos flamenco with fiery passion,
pink feathers, red dresses, they're always
in fashion!

They open their beautiful wings to the
side, their thin legs take long graceful
dance steps in stride.

The cancan the Toucans do tickles the fancy. They kick their legs high! So flashy and prancy!

Their dance is a marvelous, colorful show. It's their favorite to do, it's the best dance they know.

The Dingo fandango is danced in a ring. They circle and quick-step, they crouch and they spring.

With paws intertwined, they patter the ground, they spin like a top or a merry-go-round!

The African animals beat on
their drums, they stomp to the
rhythm and jive with their chums.

As elephants and rhinos groove
through the night, the hyenas and
lions roar with delight.

When the sun rises high,
the moon lays down its head.
It's time for each creature to
curl up in bed.

So now that you know the secret, too, enjoy this sleepy day at the zoo!

THE END

Acknowledgments

The Bell family, Lori, Gary and Whitney, Larry and Joan Kresek, Dave Collins, Hugh Alexander, Paul Yalowitz, Josh Viola and Aaron Lovett

Lindsey Bell has a BFA in illustration from Rocky Mountain College of Art and Design with an emphasis in children's book illustration. She currently instructs art classes in Westminster, Colorado.

CPSIA information can be obtained at www.ICGtesting.com
Printed in the USA
BVIW12n1255120717
488555BV00017B/276